Listening with my Heart

A STORY OF KINDNESS AND SELF-COMPASSION

By Gabi Garcia   Illustrated by Ying Hui Tan

For my friend Katherine, who brings so much love and light into the world.
And thank you Ryan-- I couldn't have done this without your support.

Copyright 2017 Gabi Garcia
Hardcover copyright 2018
gabigarciabooks.com
Illustrations by Ying Hui Tan

skinned knee
publishing
902 Gardner Road no. 4
Austin, Texas 78721

Publisher's Cataloging-in-Publication data
Names: Garcia, Gabi, author. | Tan, Ying Hui, illustrator.
Title: Listening with my heart : a story of kindness and self-compassion / by Gabi Garcia ; illustrated by Ying Hui Tan.
Description: Austin, TX: Skinned Knee Publishing, 2017.
Identifiers: ISBN 978-0-9989580-4-0 (Hardcover) | 978-0-9989580-3-3 (pbk.) | 978-0-9989580-5-7 (ebook)
Summary: A young girl realizes that it is just as important to give love and kindness to herself as it is to give it to others.
Subjects: LCSH Emotions--Juvenile fiction. | Kindness--Juvenile fiction. | Friendship--Juvenile fiction. | Empathy--Juvenile fiction. | BISAC JUVENILE FICTION / Social Themes / Emotions & Feelings.
Classification: LCC PZ7.G1556245 Li 2017 | DDC [E]--dc23

A NOTE TO PARENTS AND EDUCATORS

In today's hypercompetitive world, kids often internalize the message that their worth is attached to their accomplishments and that messing up is something to be ashamed of, rather than simply a normal part of life. This can lead to critical self-talk and kids thinking that they're not good enough. *Listening with My Heart* reminds us of the other golden rule-- to treat ourselves like we would treat a friend. When we do this, we are practicing self-compassion.

Self-compassion can support our well-being by helping to build emotional resiliency. You can help your child cultivate self-compassion by:

Helping them become aware of their emotional experiences. Encourage them to name what they're feeling and pay attention to the physical sensations that accompany their feelings. Validate their experiences and let them know that whatever they're feeling is okay.

Reminding them that disappointment, setbacks, etc. are a part of growing up. It's important for children to understand that making mistakes is normal. This doesn't mean that they aren't responsible for their actions, but they can take responsibility compassionately.

Helping them become aware of their self-talk when things don't go the way they want or expect. Critical self-talk can leave kids feeling shame, embarrassment or believing that they're not good enough. If you notice this happening with your child, ask them to think about what they'd say to a friend having the same experience. Talk about the importance of treating themselves the way they'd treat someone they care for. You can also help them find words or phrases that would feel comforting to them when they're having a hard time.

Modeling self-compassion. Kids pay attention to how we deal with our own frustrations and shortcomings. Every mistake we make is an opportunity to model kindness and compassion for ourselves.

gabigarciabooks.com for downloadable resources to accompany this book.

nly,

Esperanza's tummy fluttered as she practiced her lines on the porch. Today was the class play! Waiting for Mama to walk with her to school, she paced back and forth when she spotted a heart-shaped rock.

Esperanza picked it up and showed it to Mama as soon as she
stepped outside.
"I see you found a little treasure," said Mama.

Esperanza rubbed its rough surface and felt a twinkle of joy. "Maybe it's a sign."

"For what?" asked Mama.

She thought about the class play later that afternoon wondering what it would finally be like in the spotlight. "To put my heart into everything I do," she answered.

At that moment, they heard scratching and a soft cry. Esperanza peeked under the stairs and spotted a kitty shaking and shivering. No mama in sight. She scooped the kitten onto her lap and cuddled her. "She's all alone. I think she's hungry." Esperanza reached for her lunch bag, pinched off a piece of chicken, and offered it to the kitty, who gobbled it up.

"Mama, I think the rock is a reminder to spread kindness and love. That's what we do when we listen with our hearts."

"I think you're on to something," said Mama.

"Can we keep Cleocatra? Please?" asked Esperanza, who'd already named the kitty.

"Queens are always welcome at our house," said Mama. "If she's still here after school, we'll take her in."

At school, Esperanza was more focused on the play than on math or reading. Clutching her script during recess, she noticed Bao sitting alone on a bench. He was new in school this week and didn't speak much English. She wondered if he felt lonely or scared. Esperanza found a soccer ball and kicked it over to him.

A smile spread across Bao's face. He stood, popped the ball in the air, then bounced it between his knee and his head a few times. "Dude's got moves!" thought Esperanza.

They spent recess giggling
and making up hand signals.

Afterwards, Esperanza borrowed Ms. Owen's English - Vietnamese dictionary. She wrote "friend" in Vietnamese, drew a picture of Bao and her, then put it on his desk. Esperanza rubbed the rock in her pocket. Listening with her heart made her feel peaceful inside.

Finally, it was time for the performance! It was too late for Bao to be in the play, but he stood at Ms. Owen's side as a stage-hand.

Excitement bubbled as Esperanza awaited her cue.

Esperanza walked on stage, tripped as she was about to say her first line, and splattered across the stage.

When she got up, she forgot her lines so Ms. Owen whispered them to her from backstage. Heat rushed through Esperanza's body as all eyes were glued to her. She wished she could disappear.

"I ruined the play!" thought Esperanza, rushing off stage as soon as she'd finished her part. "I messed up in front of everyone." She tucked herself in behind some props so no one would see her.

Esperanza noticed her body shaking and her face still burning. She took a deep breath and dug the rock out of her pocket. It was cracked and lopsided, just how she felt. Esperanza touched her hand to her heart and felt the disappointment.

Bao found Esperanza a few minutes later and handed her a drawing with the word friend written above it.

Esperanza nodded. She hadn't been
treating herself like a friend.

Esperanza realized this wasn't the first time she'd been unkind to herself. At the soccer game last weekend, she'd missed the ball that swooshed by her head, and they lost the game.

"Nice work!" A player from the other team yelled as the others laughed.

Esperanza thought she'd let her team down and was the worst soccer player in the world. Thinking those thoughts had made her feel worse.

At the curtain call, Esperanza reminded herself she hadn't ruined the play. She'd had an accident, and accidents happen to everyone.

Listening with her heart wasn't just about giving kindness and love to others, it was about giving it to herself, too. I can be a friend to myself, thought Esperanza.

When Esperanza got home she focused on her favorite things. She zipped down the hill on her bike then spent the afternoon painting at the kitchen table. She also got the hug she needed from Mama, and some cuddles from Cleocatra.

LISTENING WITH YOUR HEART

Some days stink. Not everything will go the way you want. You'll get upset. When this happens, you can pause, take a few deep breaths, and practice listening with your heart. You can:

Name what you are feeling. Whatever you feel is okay.

Listen to your body. Notice the sensations you are having.

Pay attention to your self-talk. Are the words supportive and understanding or mean and rude? Are you being a friend to yourself?

When we treat ourselves with the same kindness and understanding we'd give to someone we care for, we are practicing **self-compassion**.

BEING MY OWN FRIEND

Wrap your arms around yourself and give yourself a gentle hug. Take a few deep breaths and close your eyes if you'd like. Say these words to yourself:

When I feel sadness, may I treat myself like the friend I need.
May I show love and kindness to myself.

When I feel anger, may I treat myself like the friend I need.
May I show love and kindness to myself.

(Think of feelings you experience that are difficult for you and fill in the blank.)
When I feel _____, may I treat myself like the friend I need.
May I show love and kindness to myself.

KIND WORDS FOR MYSELF

Place both hands over your heart. Notice your hands touching each other and touching your heart. Take a few deep breaths and close your eyes if you'd like.

What loving and understanding words or phrases would you like to hear when you're having a tough time or feeling upset? What would feel good or comforting to hear? Take some time and see what words or phrases come up for you. Write them down below or in a notebook and read them to yourself whenever you need to hear them.

_____
_____
_____

WE ARE ALL CONNECTED

Everyone messes up, makes mistakes, and feels strong emotions-- it's normal. Everyone also wants to feel kindness and love. This is what connects us to each other.

Place your hands gently on your lap. Take a few deep breaths and close your eyes if you'd like. Say these words to yourself:

> I connect to myself through love and kindness.
> I connect to others through love and kindness.
> I connect to the world through love and kindness.

Notice how you feel after doing these activities. You can do them whenever you want. Listening with your heart feels good. It connects you to others and reminds you to be a friend to yourself. **It helps grow a more peaceful world.**

Gabi Garcia is a mama, Licensed Professional Counselor and former teacher. She has worked as a therapist in a variety of settings for over 15 years and currently works as a public school counselor.

She writes books that support parents, educators and caregivers in nurturing mindful, socially and emotionally aware children. Gabi lives with her family in Austin, Texas.

Visit gabigarciabooks.com for free downloadable resources to accompany this book.

Other books written by Gabi Garcia
and illustrated by Ying Hui Tan

Ying Hui Tan is a children's book illustrator. You can see more of her work at yinghuitan.com.